"Shut your mouth," I yelled up at Nick. "I mean it." By then I had my fist ready.

"You and who else, farmer boy?" Nick said. Then he took a swing at me. I ducked and came up with my right under his jaw. I'm plenty strong. But I was surprised, myself, at the crunching sound and the way Nick fell back. One of the other kids caught him or he would've landed on the floor. And blood was coming from his lip, too.

When I saw the blood, I felt real strange inside, kind of sick-like. The thing is, I wanted to get him, all right, but then right after I did, I wished that I had made myself stop . . .

Boomer's Journal

by R. E. Kelley

For all the boys and girls who wrote to say how much they liked Jake's Journal, *and asked me to write another book*

Published by Worthington Press
801 94th Avenue North, St. Petersburg, Florida 33702

Copyright © 1995 by Worthington Press,
a division of PAGES, Inc.

Printed in the United States of America

2 4 6 8 10 9 7 5 3 1

ISBN 0-87406-775-8

Dear Boomer,

I'll bet when you started this journal you had no idea of all the things that were going to happen. I enjoyed reading it, and I'm glad you're letting me make it into a book.

I haven't changed your journal very much. I did add a few words here and there, so that people who don't know you or the canyon where we live will know what you are talking about. I even left some of your different words and spellings in, because the way you think and talk is part of the story.

—D

Thursday, November 12

My English teacher says everybody has to keep a journal this year. We were spozed to start last month, but I only just now got this notebook to write in.

Today I stopped by to see our neighbor, Dinah, on my way home from school. Her house is two miles up our dirt road from the bus stop, and my house is another whole mile. Dinah says I should stop and rest anytime.

I heard on the TV this morning that they are forecasting a very wet winter for southern California. It's hard to believe. All the hills

and mountains around the whole Santa
Juanita Valley are dry and brown. Out here in
Freel Canyon, it seems even drier. The only
thing green is right up close to the houses.
All the stretches in between are bare and dry.
It's too bad nobody has enough well water to
make nice pastures. It is so dry and dusty
that I was dying of thirst by the time I got to
Dinah's.

She'd just washed her hair. She wears
hardly any makeup, and with her long, dark
hair hanging down to her waist, she looked
like she was sixteen instead of twenty-six.
She'd baked oatmeal cookies. They were good,
all nice and warm. She gave me some to take

home, too. I wish Mom would make cookies like Dinah does. Maybe if she didn't work so much she would.

Dinah sure has crazy ideas about not killing things. She showed me a trap she bought to catch the ground squirrels that steal her chickens' eggs. It's like a wire box. Then she carries it back up in the canyon and lets the squirrels go. When I told Dad, he said it was the silliest thing he'd ever heard of. She should get her husband, Slim, to shoot them for her.

One reason I stopped by was to ask her if she or Slim have seen my dog. Dutch has been gone for four days now and I'm real worried.

Dad got mad at him is why he's gone. One of our little locust trees got chopped off last week. Dad knowed it was a jackrabbit that did it cuz they make a diagonal cut, just like it was with a knife.

"What's the matter with that dang Dutch, letting that jack in here by the house?" he hollered. "You're feeding him too much again, Boomer."

"I only give him one scoopful," I said.

"That's too much. He's not hungry enough to keep the rabbits away. You cut him down to half a scoop, you hear?"

"But that ain't enough for a big dog like Dutch."

"Don't argue with me, boy, if you know what's good for you."

I knowed what was good for me. When Dad makes up his mind, I watch out. I held my breath and didn't say nothing. But I guess he seen the look on my face.

"And tonight don't give him anything at all. If he's hungry he'll get that jack," he said.

"But Dad . . ."

That was as far as I got before he whacked me on the rear end. "When I tell you something you do it," he yelled. "Think you can remember that? I got enough aggravation without you." Then he gave me another whack.

There was no use arguing. I did like he said. About the third night that Dutch only got half a scoop of dry dog food, he disappeared. I spoze he went up in the mountains to find something to eat, but why ain't he come

home? Maybe that lion that almost got my pal Jake last summer got Dutch. Except for the lion, Jake and I had a lot of fun. I wish he could stay here with his dad and Dinah all the time, instead of coming only in the summer.

I told Dinah I'm scared Dutch might've gone after old Kreimer's chickens. He lives part way down the canyon. Jake and I got in trouble with him last summer. "Do you think Mr. Kreimer'd shoot him?"

"Maybe, if he caught him in with the chickens," Dinah said. "Why don't you ask him?"

I spoze I better. I stayed away from him for a time after he found out I was the one that painted <u>Kreimer is Krazy</u> on his barn door. But lately he's been giving me a ride to the Alpha-Beta supermarket when he goes to pick up old vegetables for his chickens and cows. It's only a couple of blocks from there to Canyon Junior High.

If I don't ride with him, I have to walk three miles to the school bus stop. Dad and Mom have to leave real early to get to the movie studios down in Burbank where they work so I can't ride with them, either. But if I time it right, I can catch a ride with Mr. Kreimer. He takes me from his house almost to school, and then I don't have to ride the bus with those snobs from Stone Canyon. Stone Canyon is just the other side of the hills from here in Freel Canyon, but the way they act you'd think Stone Canyon was Fifth Avenue in New York City.

That old Kreimer don't say much, but he's a tough old geezer. I've seen him heading up into the mountains with his rifle and a backpack,

just as the sun goes down. Maybe he sleeps up there some nights. I bet the coyotes take off when they see him coming. He might've seen some signs of Dutch. I sure hope he didn't catch Dutch in with his chickens, though. Dutch likes chickens, especially when he's hungry.

There's a new guy living in a trailer at Mr. Kreimer's. Sometimes he's in the truck, too, in the morning. He's a black guy. Bud Willetts.

I hope Dutch ain't gone for good. I miss him something awful. I wish Dad didn't make me cut down on his food like that.

Seems like Dad is getting meaner and meaner these last few months. He always used to yell at me and spank me when I done something wrong. Now lately it seems like he gets mad real easy and whacks me for no reason at all. He says I'm aggravating him. I try to stay away from him as much as I can, especially when Mom's not home. When she's here she sticks up for me and then he gets mad at her.

I found out what happened to Dutch. Old Kreimer knew, all right.

"I saw him. Shot him," he said.

"You <u>shot</u> him?" I couldn't believe he'd admit it, flat out like that.

"Had to. He was too far gone. Had to put him out of his misery," he said.

"What do you mean?"

Bud was sitting between us, so Mr. Kreimer couldn't see me, but my voice sounded funny. He must've known I was crying. He said, "Boy, you don't want to know."

"Yes, I do. What was wrong with my dog?"

"He was blind. Must've been blundering around trying to find his way home. Might've been homing in on my cows' bellerings."

"He'd have been all right once I got him home where he knew his way around," I told him. "Why'd you go and shoot him without even asking?"

"That ain't all that was wrong, boy. You sure you want to know?"

"I gotta know."

Then old Kreimer said, "His belly was ripped open. His guts were hanging out. Must have been in a terrible fight. He was more dead than alive, son. I saved him a few more hours of misery is all."

Bud put his arm around me. He must've felt me shaking cuz he pulled me over against his shoulder. I leaned against him and wiped my eyes on my sleeve. "You got any other dogs?" Bud asked.

"Nope. No dogs. Nor cats, either. Coyotes got our cats."

"Any brothers or sisters?" He squeezed

my shoulder.

"Nope. Just Dutch."

"That's tough." I never knew any black guys before. I like Bud. He's got a bad leg from the war, but he gets around okay. He and Mr. Kreimer were buddies in the marines. He's from Boston. When he talks, he sounds like my grandma.

Grandma died, just a couple months ago. She lived in Connecticut. Bud says that's in the same neck of the woods as Boston.  Grandma's lawyer sent me a videocassette that Grandma made for me before she died. Dinah let me play it on her VCR.

It's funny, I didn't think I remembered Grandma at all. I lived with her after my real mother died in the accident. When I was real little. I was only three when Dad got married again and I came to live here with him and Mom. But when I saw Grandma on the video,

I remembered her all over again.

She says she is leaving her money to me so I can go to college or trade school. In the meantime, I get an allowance of $50 a month. I can buy anything I want with it, or I can save it up for a car or something. But it's not spozed to be for food or clothes or nothing else like that. Not for anything that a parent normally provides, she says on the tape.

Dad got mad as a hornet when he heard about that. He really told the lawyer off on the phone, but it didn't do any good. The lawyer has all the say about how Grandma's money is spent for me. He told Dad that if Dad didn't want me to get the money, Dad didn't have to the sign the papers that were coming in the mail.

Dad signed all right. I'm going to save $40 every month. So far I got $80 in a cigar box under my bed. Maybe by next summer when my friend Jake is back, I'll have enough and I can buy a dirt bike and we can ride around the canyon. I wish it was summer again already. I get lonesome, especially without Dutch. My folks are gone from early in the morning till after dark every night. Mom always has something I can warm up in the microwave, but I get tired of eating alone.

Monday, December 7

Today Mr. Coburn asked me how I was doing on my journal, so I better write some more.

Dinah gave me a ride home from the bus stop this afternoon. She asked me if I could give her a hand for a few minutes. She is going to have a baby and isn't spozed to do any wheelbarrowing. It was a surprise to me. She don't look fat yet. I helped her load up the wheelbarrow with grain and scratch and pushed it over to the chicken pen for her.

She was going to pay me, but I said I'd rather have some of her cookies. She was all

19

out of cookies, so she gave me a loaf of homemade bread instead. I'm going to stop by three times a week after school to do some chores for her, and she is going to pay me.

Slim is working long hours at the studio. Dinah says they're shooting a big Western. Slim and all the other wranglers that handle the horses are real busy. Slim doesn't get home until after dark. I guess the studios are pretty busy, cuz my folks are in props and they don't get home until real late, either.

With my allowance from Grandma, I don't need Dinah to pay me. I already got $120 stashed away toward a motorcycle. I would help out Dinah anyway. After all, Jake is my best friend, even if he's only here with Dinah and Slim in the summer. But Dinah says she will feel better about telling me what to do if she pays me. So now I have a real job.

That's not my only good news. Last Friday, when Mr. Kreimer and Bud gave me a ride to school, Bud told me to stop by on my way home. When I got there that afternoon, Bud gave me a puppy! She's a Golden Retriever. I call her Sunny because she is such a bright golden red, like the sun. She is the best dog in the world. She's not even half grown-up and she's already housebroken. I promised Bud I would be sure she had plenty to eat so she don't have to go hunting in the mountains by herself.

Mr. Kreimer says the Alpha-Beta some-times throws out cottage cheese that's too old to sell but good enough to eat. Whenever he gets some, he'll leave a carton in our mail-box for me to give Sunny. He says growing dogs need calcium and cottage cheese is good for them. I found some in the mailbox Saturday and Sunny gobbled it down.

Dad don't think much of Golden Retrievers. He says they are too yellow-livered to be good watch dogs. Sunny slept in my room Friday night, when I first got her. Mom knowed about her, but not Dad. He was drinking again. He didn't even see Sunny until Saturday. Then there was an awful ruckus.

"I'm not feeding any worthless dogs," he said when he saw her that morning. "Any dogs around here gotta earn their keep. That pup's too fat already."

"I'll pay for her food," I told him. "I promised Bud Willetts I'd feed her good. So she don't have to hunt up in the mountains and get killed like Dutch."

"You saying it's my fault Dutch got killed?" Dad yelled. He'd been drinking some ever since he got out of bed. He grabbed me by the arm like he was going to hit me.

Mom came in the house to see what he was yelling about. "What's going on here?" She came over and stood next to me.

"None of your dang business, woman. Keep out of it," he said, but he let go of my arm.

"This is my house, too, Chuck Nichols. I got a right to know what's going on," she yelled back at him.

"You and this danged brat in it together, ain't you! I might've knowed," he hollered.

Then Mom told me to take Sunny and go

22

on outside, that she and Dad had something to settle. They had an awful row, Dad yelling and Mom crying. After a while Dad went stomping out of the house and took off in the pickup. When I went in, Mom was in their room.

I called through the door, "You all right, Mom?"

"I'm okay now. I'll be out in a little bit."

I made us some tuna fish sandwiches and after a while she came out and ate with me. Her hair was all mussed up and there was a bright red spot on the side of her face. She put her arm around my shoulder. Sometimes I think she cares more about me than my dad does, even if she is my stepmother. When he's drinking, I don't think Dad cares about me at all. Seems like he thinks I'm trying to do things that make him mad, but I ain't.

Mom said I can keep Sunny. When Dad came home Sunday, he just kind of ignored Sunny, so I guess he is going to let me keep her. He didn't say so but I think he was sorry that he acted so mean and rough when he was drunk. He brought me a couple of motorcycle magazines. I already had one of them, but I didn't tell him that.

Mr. Kreimer and Bud Willetts went some-place today on account of it's Pearl Harbor Day. I had to take the bus to school. By the time I got on, most all the seats were taken by the rich snobs who live up Stone Canyon. Nobody moved over to make room. They think they're better than everybody else, with their big houses and expensive clothes and fancy hair. The girls are so stuck-up, I can't stand them. The boys give me a pain. And the snotty remarks they make I can do without. They act like they're better than anybody who don't live in Stone Canyon. I hope Mr. Kreimer is back so I can ride with him tomorrow.

Coming home ain't so bad because our bus is a second bus. We have to wait for twenty-five minutes at school. The rich brats don't like to wait and some of them get their folks to pick them up. So it isn't so crowded, and I can even get a seat by myself sometimes.

I wish I could take Sunny to school. I don't know any kids in junior high except for the snobby brats from Stone Canyon that were in my grade school. They don't want to be friends with me, and I don't want to be friends with them.

Wednesday, December 9

My folks still aren't home and it's too dark out to go outside. There is something wrong with the TV so I might as well write in this journal.

I usually play with Sunny, but tonight she is sacked out on my bed. I stopped by to do chores for Dinah this afternoon. She invited me to stay for dinner. She said Slim is going to Mexico on location next week. He's going to be gone until Christmas. She asked, "Would you like to stay over here with me?"

"I don't know."

"Think about it. With your folks working long hours, you must not see much of them. Maybe you and I could keep each other company."

When I left she gave me a bunch of scraps for Sunny. So Sunny had an extra big dinner, and now she is sleeping it off.

I wrote a story for my English class about Sunny and how I got her. I guess writing this journal <u>has</u> made writing easier. Or maybe it's cuz I was writing about Sunny. Anyhow, I got an "A." It's the first "A" I ever got in English. Mr. Coburn wrote a note on my paper asking me to come in after school.

When I got there he said he liked my story a lot, even if I had some trouble with the grammar and spelling. He said he liked the way I had a lot of dialogue. (That's probably cuz I used to read so many comic books, but I didn't tell him that!) He said it's good to use people talking in stories and it's okay to write the words like people say them. But if it's not somebody talking I ain't, I mean AM NOT, spozed to write "ain't."

He said the important thing about writing is to learn how to get your ideas across. The grammar and stuff can always be fixed. We're spozed to write in our journals every day. I told him I would write more pages when I had something to write about. Every day is too boring. He said okay.

But the best thing is, he gave me a library pass for after school. Now when I wait for the bus, I can wait in the school library and read. He must've told the librarian something, cuz when I showed her my pass today, she right away had the latest <u>Ranger Rick</u> magazines on her desk for me to look at. And she showed me where she keeps the motorcycle magazines and where books about dinosaurs are cuz I told her those were my favorites. The library's got a lot of them I never read.

While I was reading, a girl with red hair came and sat at my table. She has a pony-tail that is as long as Dinah's braids and is it ever red! I could hardly keep from giving it a yank, but I didn't want to lose my library pass.

So I just smiled at her. She smiled back and said, "Hi, I'm Mary Margaret Murphy."

"I'm Charles Nichols, but people call me Boomer. Gosh, Mary Margaret was my mother's name. What a coincidence."

"Oh, did she die? I'm sorry."

"It was a long time ago. I live with my dad and stepmother now, out in Freel Canyon."

"I know where that is. I live in Stone Canyon," she said.

I was surprised to hear that, all right. "I never see you on the bus."

"I hate the bus! I hate those stuck-up girls."

I laughed. "Me, too. And the boys are nerds. I get a ride with a neighbor in the morning, so I only have to ride the bus home."

"My mom works here in the school office, and I ride with her." Just then a big kid with thick black hair came in the door and she waved to him. "Patrick rides with us, too. He goes to high school."

I had to hurry to catch my bus, so I got up. The big guy took my place. I heard him say, "Hi, Red." She smiled up at him like she really likes him.

I wonder how come he rides home with her? He can't be her brother cuz he talks with a kind of an accent. When he said "Red," it sounded more like "Rrred." She's in seventh grade, same as me. She shouldn't have a boyfriend that old.

I wonder if she would get mad if I gave her a ribbon for her ponytail? Grandma's lawyer

has already sent me $50 each for October and November and December. Besides the $120 in the cigar box under my bed, I still got most of the other $30 which I saved out for spending money. I'm going to use it for Christmas presents. I bet a green ribbon would look pretty with her red hair. And it would look like Christmas, too. I bet she'd like it, but what if her big boyfriend got mad?

Tomorrow I'm going to write to Grandma's lawyer. This is my practice, so I can get it just right and just copy it tomorrow:

Dear Mr. Hotchkins,
Thank you for sending me the three checks for $50, for October and November and December. I'm gonna save $40 every month until I have enough for a motorcycle. I am having a hard time finding a safe place to keep it here at my house. And it is hard for me to get to a bank. Do you think you could just send me $10 a month, and save the other $40 for me until next summer?

Yr frnd, Boomer
(Charles B. Nichols, Jr.)

That looks okay, I guess. I don't want to tell what really happened this afternoon. Mom was gone to the store and Dad was drinking a lot. I was reading a motorcycle magazine in my room, thinking about what kind I'd like to have. I felt like counting the $120. I reached under the bed and got my cigar box. It was empty. I looked all under the bed, but the money was gone.

A couple of nights ago, I'd heard Mom complaining that Dad had spent all the grocery money on booze. But when she left to go to the store after lunch, I'd seen him hand her a couple of twenties. And he'd had more in his wallet, too.

I worked for Dinah all this morning. I had a pretty good idea of what had happened while I was over there.

"Dad, I'm missing $120. It was in a cigar box under my bed. You got it?" I asked him.

"What if I have?"

"It's my money. I'm saving it for a motor-cycle."

"No way! That's food money. You're living here, eating off me. Why shouldn't you help pay for your food?"

"Cuz Grandma said it's for extra things, things I want special. Gimme it back." I reached toward his wallet.

"You good-for-nothing little bum." He started shaking me.

Sunny didn't like that. She grabbed his leg. Dad let go of me real fast. He reached down and put his hands around Sunny's throat. He was going to strangle her! "I'll teach you to come after me, you and your miserable dog," he yelled.

"Stop! Stop! You can have the money! Put her down!"

Just as he let go of Sunny, the kitchen door opened and Mom came in with the groceries. "What's going on here? What money?" She looked

34

at me. "Did he take your motorcycle money?"

I grabbed up Sunny and nodded.

"You better go to your room, Boomer. I'll see you get your money back."

Then she lit into Dad something awful. I didn't know she knowed those words. And what he said was worse, only he didn't stop at just words. I could hear him hitting her. I went running out to help her.

She hollered, "You killed your first wife, Chuck Nichols, driving when you were soused to the gills. Well, you're not gonna kill me."

She ran into the kitchen and reached for the rifle Dad keeps there. "Give the kid his money, Chuck, or I'll use this right where it will hurt most." She was breathing hard and shaking, but her voice was quiet and calm.

Dad swore something awful, but he handed over the money from his wallet.

"Count it, Boomer," Mom said.

"There's $82."

"I'll see you get the rest of it." Then she waved the gun at Dad. "Now get out of my sight. Come back when you're sober and have some common decency."

After he left, Mom went in her room and shut the door. She cried and cried. I did, too. Sunny knows something is wrong. She licked my face, and now she is cuddled up to me on my bed. Mom is still crying.

Yesterday morning, Mom's eyes were all puffed up and red. Her lip was swollen, and I could see a cut on the side of her mouth. She didn't say anything about it, though, so I didn't either.

After breakfast, she broke the bad news. "We're leaving, Boomer. We're gonna stay at my friend's In the Valley. Pack up your clothes. She's coming for us at eleven."

"What about Sunny? Can she come?"

"I'm afraid not. Irene lives in an apartment where they don't allow dogs."

"If Sunny can't go, I gotta stay here with her."

"Maybe Mr. Willetts would take her back."

"I don't want him to take her back. She's just about my best friend in the whole world. I'll stay here with her."

"Not with your father, you won't!"

"I'll stay with Dinah. Slim's going to Mexico until Christmas. Dinah already invited me."

"You're not just saying that?"

"Honest. You can call her," I said.

She gave me a big argument, crying and everything. I could tell she wanted me to come with her, even if I'm not really her son at all. And I sure hated to see her go. But I wouldn't go if Sunny couldn't.

"Just 'til Christmas, Boomer. When Slim gets back," she said, when she got in Irene's car.

At least this year I have money to buy Christmas presents. Then, after Christmas, I'm going to try to save most of the $10 the lawyer sends me. I'm still working for Dinah and saving that money, too. I hope I can get a dirt bike in July when Jake comes. We can ride all over our canyon, and maybe over to

Stone Canyon to see Mary Margaret. I see her almost every day in the library. That big guy I thought was her boyfriend is her cousin, Patrick Shanley. He's from Ireland. He's okay.

Dad came home yesterday afternoon. After he read Mom's note, he said, "She says you didn't want to go with her."

"I told her Dinah wants me to stay with her while Slim is gone."

"Well, Slim isn't going after all," Dad said. "I just met him on the road. He said the shooting schedule has been changed, and they're not going on location until after the holidays." Dad got a funny look on his face. Almost as if he was crying. "Maybe you'll want to go with Mom after all."

"No, I better stay here." I didn't say it was on account of Sunny.

Then he smiled. "So it's you and me against the world, ain't it, Boomer." He put his arm around my shoulder. "Let's go out for pizza." And we went. Dad was real nice and friendly. I was glad I hadn't told him that the real reason I decided not to go was Sunny.

I sure hope Mom comes back soon. I'm trying real hard not to do anything aggravating. Me and Dad are getting along okay so far, but I don't know how long it will last.

Friday, December 18

After school yesterday, Mr. Coburn gave me a paperback dictionary for a Christmas present. I didn't have anything to give him. I felt bad. He said maybe I could write him another story, maybe about Sunny or about Christmas. I spoze maybe I will.

It will give me something to do over vacation if it keeps on raining so much. Bud Willetts says his bum leg tells him it's going to be a wet winter. Mr. Kreimer says we're about due for a flood.

I'm doing some extra work for Dinah this

week. With all this rain, there is a lot of cleaning up to do. She sure is nice. I told her about wanting to buy a green ribbon for Mary Margaret for Christmas. She picked me up at school the next day and we went shopping. I wound up buying a pretty scarf, in all different colors of green. Kind of like the ocean. Then Dinah wrapped it up fancy for me.

I was planning to give it to Mary Margaret today, the last day before vacation. But on Wednesday, when we were in the library, she whispered, "Are you going to the Christmas dance after school tomorrow?"

"I don't think so," I said.

"How come? I'm going. We could go together."

I'd been thinking she was probably going to go with one of those guys with the fancy clothes from Stone Canyon, so I was plenty surprised when she said she'd go with me. "All right. I'd like to go with you," I told her. There wasn't going to be a late bus. But even if I had to walk the six miles home it would be worth it, I figured.

"Good," she said. Then she reached right

out and put her hand on mine. I was embarrassed, but we were the only kids in the library,
and the librarian was behind one of the shelves.
Mary Margaret gave me a little smile, as
though she might be embarrassed, too.

She said, "I've been hoping you'd go with
me, Charlie." She always calls me "Charlie."
That's what Grandma called me, too.

"I've never been to a dance," I told her.
"What are we spozed to wear?"

"I've never been to one, either. I asked my
mom. She says regular school clothes are
fine."

"I've got something you might like to wear.
Wait a minute." I ran to my locker and got
the package Dinah had wrapped for me.

Boy, was she surprised! When she
unwrapped it, I could tell she really liked it, too.

Yesterday, just before we went to the dance, she undid her pony tail and tied the scarf around her head. It looked all flowing and soft, the scarf and her hair together. She looked real pretty and Christmasy. A lot of kids gave us the eye when we walked into the gym together. I wore my best boots. With the heels, I was almost as tall as she was.

I danced with some girls and she danced with a lot of other boys, but she always kept coming back to dance with me. And when it was all over, her mother gave me a ride home. I tried to get her to drop me off at the end of the paved road where the school bus stops, but she drove all the way up the dirt road to my house.

It was late when we got here, dinnertime. I was glad it was dark. I've never seen her house, but those houses in Stone Canyon are pretty fancy. I don't spoze my house looks like much compared to hers. And Dad's car was here, too. I hoped he wouldn't come out and he didn't.

It probably would have been all right even if

he had. He seemed like he was in good shape. He'd brought home a thick steak for our dinner and an apple pie from the bakery. He teased me about having a girlfriend, but I didn't mind. I didn't tell him about buying her a scarf, though. He's funny about that money I get from Grandma.

I think Mary Margaret is a real neat girl. She has a horse and so does Patrick. They are going to ride over during Christmas vacation, now that she knows where I live. I hope they don't come when I am working over at Dinah's.

I sure wish Mom would come back. I miss her a lot, even if she isn't my real mother. When she called Wednesday and found out Slim didn't go to Mexico after all, she was all set to try to borrow a car and come get me. But I told her I had new friends at school and Dad and I were getting along real good and she shouldn't worry.

Then she talked to Dad and I heard him say, "He's my son and if he wants to stay here, he's going to stay here. His grandmother couldn't get him away from me, and you can't either." Then he motioned for me to go in my room. For a long time he talked real low so I couldn't hear. I think Dad wants Mom to come back as much as I do. He has hardly been drinking at all. Me and Mom and Dad are all going to go to a restaurant for Christmas dinner. I hope it works out.

Wednesday, December 23

I'm going to write another letter. This is practice:

Dear Mr. Hotchkins,
Thank you for opening a bank account for me, to put the money in every month. It is a good idea, like you wrote. And like you said, the interest will help, too, cuz I'm trying to save enough to buy a good used motorcycle this summer.
Now that I got my Christmas presents all bought, I won't be needing as much money. And besides, I have a job for a

neighbor three days a week. Please start putting $45 in the bank account for me. Send me only $5. I really want a motorcycle more than anything cuz then I can ride all around our canyon.

Yr frnd, Boomer

I guess that's okay. I sure hope I can save enough.

Saturday, December 26

I wish the dang rain would stop. It's been raining all Christmas vacation. Dad is worrying about floods if it keeps up like this much longer. Last Sunday, we dug a ditch to channel the water away from our house and barn. We worked all day until it started to pour again around four o'clock. It was hard work. And Dad had a hangover. That didn't help none, either.

It was cold out but the sweat was running down my face. When dirt is wet like it is now, shoveling is hard work. "Why don't we get the tractor fixed?" I asked.

"That piece of junk? Cost almost as much to fix it as it would to get a new one. Besides, that ain't heavy enough. We oughtta have a bigger one, a new one."

"Why don't we get one?"

"You think it'd be a good idea, then?" He had a funny look on his face.

"Anything's better than this," I said. "Besides, I'd like to drive a tractor. I could maybe even get jobs with it. Like clearing brush and plowing fields."

"Yeah, you could make good money. That's an idea." He stopped and rested on his shovel for a couple of minutes. Then he said, "I'll think about it." The rain started coming down hard then and we had to quit, but he seemed like he was in a better mood all the rest of the afternoon and dinnertime, too. He even found some pork chops in the freezer and fixed a big dinner with sauerkraut and apple sauce and baked potatoes. He's almost as good a cook as Mom.

But our Christmas dinner with Mom yesterday didn't work out. The food was good.

We had goose and plum pudding and some other things I never tried before. My folks didn't talk much, though. After we ate, Mom gave me a new motorcycle magazine to read while I waited for them in the car. When they came out, I could see Mom had been crying. Dad looked pale. He had an awful look on his face.

On the way home, he stopped to buy some liquor. When we got home, I pretended I had a bellyache and went in my room with Sunny and went to bed.

I feel sorry for Dad sometimes. When he's not drinking, he can be real nice. He'd been off the booze for almost a week, until we had dinner with Mom last night.

Yesterday morning was Christmas morning. He said, "Here's the money I owe you, son." He handed me three twenties.

"You only owed me $38."

"The rest is interest."

I knew the interest wouldn't be that much. He was just trying to make up for what happened that weekend when Mom left. But I only said, "Thanks a lot."

"And here's something else you may be needing," he said. He brought out a big box with a motorcycle helmet in it! It's a beaut! The real expensive kind, with a visor and face guard. Wow! Some Christmas present.

I can hardly wait until summer when I can get my dirt bike. But right now, I would be happy if this rain would just let up. It's still coming down in buckets tonight. Mr. Kreimer says this is the most rain we've ever had in December since he's been keeping track with his rain gauge. I'm glad me and Dad dug that ditch.

Wednesday, December 30

Dad had me write a letter to Mr. Hotchkins about using Grandma's money for a tractor. I wonder if he will say yes. I would really rather have a motorcycle.

I'm glad Christmas vacation is almost over. We've had so much rain. It's boring staying in the house. I was sure glad when I had some company yesterday. Dad didn't have to work, but he'd gone to the store because the rain had let up. I was in the barn when Sunny started barking her head off at two horses coming in our driveway. It was Mary Margaret and Patrick. I shushed Sunny and told her it was all right. She trotted along behind me then, just like I been training her to do.

"We were going to come sooner, but every time we got ready to come, it started to rain," Mary Margaret said.

"I'm glad you made it today." I helped her down from her horse. We tied the horses up and I showed her and Patrick around. She slipped her hood back, and I could see she had the green scarf I gave her tied around her ponytail.

Patrick must've seen me noticing it cuz he said, "She wears it all the time."

"I do not. Besides, why shouldn't I? You're the one who keeps telling me Irish people should wear green." She was blushing. Maybe I was, too. She reached down to pat Sunny. Sunny almost went crazy. Since I got her, it's the first time anybody else besides me has been so nice to her.

"She's a pedigreed Golden Retriever. Watch her retrieve." I got her favorite old shoe and threw it. Sunny raced to get it and brought it right back.

"Here. See if she'll retrieve for you." I handed Patrick the shoe and he threw it. She brought it back to him, and he kept throwing it and throwing it. Me and Mary Margaret went off to the side a little.

"I'm glad you came," I said. "When you didn't come for so long, I thought you might be mad at me or something."

"I wanted to come see you, Charlie. But last week I had to help my mom get ready for Christmas. And it's been raining all the time ever since."

"It's going to start in again pretty soon, by the looks of things." I sure didn't want them to go, but I was afraid they'd be in real trouble if it started pouring down hard again. It was already thundering.

Mary Margaret looked up at the sky. "Yeah, we better start back." She untied her horse. "A man waved to us when we came over the hill. By a house and a trailer, on the other side of the big wash. A black man."

"That's Bud, the guy who gave me Sunny.

He lives in the trailer. Mr. Kreimer that gives me a ride to school in the morning lives in the house. He and Bud were in the marines together."

"The marines? My dad's a marine! He works in the recruiting office downtown. And Patrick's going to be a marine when he gets out of school."

Patrick came over and untied his horse. "What's that you're a-sayin' about me?" I found out he only came to this country from Ireland when he was twelve. That's why he talks a little different.

Mary Margaret explained about Bud and Mr. Kreimer both being marines. She said maybe they'd stop and say hello on the way back, but Patrick said they'd be lucky if they got home before the rain started as it was.

I hated to see them go, but the sky was getting darker and darker. Patrick was right. In a little while it was pouring again. I'll be glad when it stops raining. If there's a flood, I'm not sure the ditch me and Dad dug will hold it.

The rains finally stopped and I was glad to be going back to school. But now I wish it was still Christmas vacation. Seems like everything went wrong this week. I didn't even feel like writing.

Monday, during P. E., somebody stole my lunch money, so I didn't have any lunch.

Then, after school, Mary Margaret told me that Patrick is going to be in a play at the high school. He has to go to rehearsals after school every day. Mary Margaret's mother is going to wait after school for him, so Mary

Margaret is spozed to ride the bus home.

When she lined up for the bus with me, this big blond eighth-grader started making up to her and telling her he really liked redheads. I hadn't seen him on the afternoon bus before. Probably his mother usually picks him up.

He was right behind us and when we got to our seats he said, "Watch out, hick, I'm sitting here." He tried to push me away so he could sit next to Mary Margaret.

"No, Charlie's sitting with me," she said, taking my arm. "Don't mind Nick," she said to me as he sat down right behind her. "Just because his dad's on the school board, he acts like he owns the bus."

The guy gave her ponytail a tug. "Watch it, my little Red-y Head-y."

The look on his face and the way he said it made me mad, but Mary Margaret only said, "You cut that out, Nick Sherman." She said it that way girls do when they don't really mean it.

"Leave her alone, nerd," I said.

He grabbed me by my shirt collar from

behind. "You calling me a nerd, farmer boy?"

"Nick, stop it right this minute or I'll never speak to you again," Mary Margaret said.

She raised her voice enough so the bus driver hollered, "What's going on back there?" So Nick let go of me and settled back in his seat.

For once I was sorry that my stop is the first one. As I was walking down the aisle toward the door, Nick said, "Anybody got a bottle of Lysol? This seat oughtta be cleaned." I looked back and he had moved up to sit with Mary Margaret. I could tell she was answering him back, but I couldn't hear what she said.

The next day, Tuesday, was just as bad. Maybe worse. Nick sat right behind us again on the way home. He wasn't as mouthy, mostly joking about the teachers. Mary Margaret kept laughing at his wisecracks. He had some funny names for them, all right, but it seemed to me she was laughing and turning around and smiling at him more than she needed to. When I got up to get off, he moved up to sit with her. "Are you Redy for me, Heady?" The smart aleck way he said it made me want to slug him, but Mary Margaret acted like she thought it was funny.

On Wednesday, I didn't see her in school all day. Yesterday, I tried to talk to her during school, but I couldn't. She has first lunch and I have second, and we don't have any classes together. When I saw her between classes, she said, "Oh, Charlie, I've got to rush." She didn't come to the library after school. And she wasn't on the bus.

Today I didn't see her to talk to during school, either. I think she was ducking me. But I knew where her last class was, so as soon as the final bell rang, I raced over there to catch her.

"I've been missing you in the library. And you weren't on the bus, either," I said.

"I was sick Wednesday. And I'm not riding the bus anymore." She moved as though she wanted to get away from me, but i put my arm up against the wall in front of her.

"Is it that Nick? Is he your boyfriend now?"

"No! No, he's not!" She almost spat it out.

"Then what's the matter? Did I do something? How come you aren't in the library? Don't you like me anymore?"

"It's not you, Charlie."

"What's the matter, then?"

"Oh, nothing. I've just decided to walk up and wait for Patrick and my mom in the high school library."

"Can't you wait in the library here?"

"It closes too soon. It's just easier to go on up there. My mom fixed it so I can go in the library there."

"I still don't see why you don't go to the library here for a while, like we always did. What's wrong?"

She looked in my eyes. Her eyes were wet and shiny, almost crying. "Honest, Charlie, it's not you. It's me."

"Well, at least you could tell me what it is."

She must have seen how bad I felt cuz she said, "Maybe I'll ride over to your house this weekend. We can play with Sunny. Okay?"

And that is all I got out of her. I'm afraid she won't come tomorrow. I think it is all over between us. And it's all the fault of that dang Nick Sherman. Come to think of it, he hasn't been on the bus, either. His mother must be picking him up again.

I wish I knew more about girls. I thought Mary Margaret and I were going along fine, and now look what's happened.

Sunday, January 10

I found out what was wrong with Mary Margaret. She showed up yesterday about eleven. Just her and her horse, Tinker.

"Patrick's gone to a rehearsal. I brought some sandwiches for our lunch," she said.

"How about we take Sunny for a hike up the canyon?"

"Will Tinker be okay here by himself?" she asked.

"My dad's in the house. Nobody'll bother your horse. I'll go tell him." I didn't tell her Dad was still in bed and that I just left him a note.

I was pretty sure he'd been drinking the night before. He's grumpy when he has a hangover and I didn't want to wake him up.

Mary Margaret's a good hiker. She said she and Patrick used to live along a big canyon down by the marine base at Camp Pendleton and they did a lot of hiking.

After all the rains, the water coming down the canyon behind our house made a pretty good stream. It made a trickling sound. Mary Margaret said it was almost like music. The sun was out and everything was green and bright.

When we got to the spring, we ate the sandwiches. "I hope you like peanut butter on your bologna sandwiches," she said.

"Sounds weird." I took a bite. "But it tastes good. You always make them this way?"

"Yeah."

Then it seemed like there wasn't anything to say for a while. Even after we finished eating, we both just sat there, watching the stream tumble down over the rocks. I was feeling all relaxed and happy, but when I looked over at her I saw a tear on her cheek.

"What's the matter, Mary Margaret?"

She shook her head and brushed away the tear. It made me all shaky inside to see her crying, but I didn't know what to say. I waited.

Finally she asked, "Charlie, can you keep a secret?"

"Sure."

"I just gotta tell somebody. But if I tell my mom or dad, that'll make it even worse. And I'm not even sure I can tell you." I waited for her to go on, but she sat quiet, like she was thinking.

Finally I said, "Is it about Nick Sherman? Or why you didn't come to school Wednesday? Were you sick or something?"

"Or something, you could call it. And it was Nick Sherman." She turned her head and looked at me. "Remember Tuesday, when he started acting nicer on the bus?"

"Yeah, and you were acting like you liked him."

She blinked and put her head down. "That was the trouble," she said, her voice real low.

"When we got off the bus, he carried my books to my house. We went around in back. I unlocked the kitchen door. Then . . . then. . . he said he thought he should get a little reward for carrying my books. I said I'd get him a Coke. He said that wasn't what he meant. He grabbed my arms and pushed me up against the wall and started kissing me. It was awful. He had me shoved up against the wall so tight I couldn't get away. I finally got a leg up and stomped on his foot. I stomped so hard, he loosened his grip and I broke away." Mary Margaret dabbed at her eyes. "And Boomer, he . . . he . . . he <u>laughed</u> at me like I was some kind of trashy joke. It was just awful."

She turned and looked at me again. Tears were running down her face. "If my dad ever finds out, he'll make a fuss that the whole school will hear about."

"I'll never tell him."

"I know you won't, Charlie. You're the only person I could tell about it."

"Then why did you stay away from me? You went rushing away from me like you were mad.

You didn't even come to the library anymore."

"Because I felt so awful, so . . . kind of cheap. It makes me feel awful just talking about it." Her voice was so low I could hardly hear her. "I didn't want anybody to know about it."

"There's nothing so awful about kissing."

"There is if you're kissing the wrong person!" she bawled.

"Well, anyway, it wasn't your fault. Don't feel bad. I think you're just about the nicest girl I ever knew, Mary Margaret. But I would never kiss you if you didn't want me to. Would I be a wrong person, too?"

She looked me straight in the eyes and even smiled a little. "No, you're not the wrong person at all."

So I kissed her. She has the kind of lips that look like a famous sculptor carved them. I was surprised how soft and nice they felt. And how they just sort of fitted with mine.

We talked some more. She is going to give me riding lessons every weekend. I'm not all that crazy about riding horses. Motorcycles are better. But it will be a good way for me to see her, away from school and the bus and everything. She gave me the first lesson on Tinker when we got back to my house.

Later, when she and Dad were both gone, a Mr. Banks called. He said he's a friend of Mr. Hotchkins. He is coming to see me this afternoon. I wonder what it is about.

Monday, January 11

That Mr. Banks showed up yesterday afternoon. I thought he would be an old guy, but he looked more like my dad. Except he was all dressed up, like he was going to church or something.

He came in a Honda. "If I'd known about your road, Boomer, I would have rented a four-wheel drive," he said. He had that same kind of accent as Grandma and Bud Willetts.

"It's bad right now on account of the rain," I told him.

"What does your father drive?" He looked

around the yard. "Is he here now?"

"He's got a four-wheel drive Toyota. It makes it okay. But he's not here today."

"Oh? I was hoping to talk to him, too. Does he know I'm going to be here today?"

"He didn't get home last night, so I didn't get a chance to tell him."

One eyebrow went up, but Mr. Banks didn't say anything. He reached down and patted Sunny. When he stood up again,

he said, "How about showing me around a little? When Mr. Hotchkins heard I was coming out here for a conference, he asked me to stop in and see how you are."

He threw a stick for Sunny to chase. "My boy, Joey, has a Retriever, too. As long as Joey keeps throwing, Laddie will keep retrieving. Is your dog like that?"

"She sure is."

"Your grandmother was a fine lady." He

reached down and took the stick from Sunny and threw it for her again. "Mr. Hotchkins wants to do what's right for you, Boomer. But it's hard for him to know, being so far away. That's why he asked me to come have a look-see."

I took him all around the barn and the well house and everything. I saw him looking at all the whiskey bottles in our trash barrels, but he didn't say anything. I showed him the ditch me and Dad dug to keep the water from going in the house and barn. "Our tractor's broke. We had to dig this all by hand," I told him.

"What's wrong with the tractor?"

"Burned out. It ran out of oil and got ruined."

"Was it your idea or your father's to use some of your money for a new tractor?" he asked.

"My dad's. But it's okay with me. I probably won't want to go to college, anyhow. And if we had a big tractor, I could maybe even get brush-clearing jobs with it."

"I see."

"Do you want to come in the house? My dad

has a catalog. I could show you the one he wants to get. You could have a cup of coffee."

"Would your stepmother mind? I don't want to intrude."

"She's not here any more. She moved out before Christmas."

"Oh," he said, and that eyebrow went up again. "Yes, perhaps a cup of coffee would be a good idea before I start back."

He didn't seem much interested in the tractor catalog, though. He asked a lot of questions about when Dad worked, how much he was gone, who fixed my meals, and things like that. After a while he asked, "What sub-ject do you like best in school?"

"English. I like my English teacher best. He got me a library pass." So then I had to explain what a library pass was. "I've already read most of the books about dinosaurs. Now I'm reading all the National Geographics."

"Sounds like you might want to be an anthropologist or archeologist someday," he said.

"What's the difference?"

72

"An anthropologist studies different kinds of peoples and cultures to see the different ways they have of coping with life. Like in Indian or African tribes. An archeologist studies the same thing, but in ancient peoples who lived long ago."

"You mean like when they dig things up and find old pots and bones and stuff? I'd like that. How do you get to be one of those?"

"You'd have to go to college. What kind of grades do you get, Boomer?"

"Depends. Mostly A's in English and History. I like them. The rest, mostly B's and C's."

"It's important for a man to find a job that he likes, doing work he enjoys. Your father wrote to Mr. Hotchkins that he could get you into the studio drivers union if you learned to operate a tractor."

He pulled a paper from his pocket. "In this letter to Mr. Hotchkins you mention working for the studios, too. Do you think that's what you want to do when you get out of school?"

"It'll be all right." I never really thought that much about it but I didn't tell him that.

He showed me the paper. It was a copy of the letter I wrote Mr. Hotchkins asking if I could use my grandma's money to buy a tractor because it would help me get a job when I get out of school. "Did you write this letter, Boomer?"

"Sure, I wrote it. I signed my name, didn't I?"

"But your father told you what words to write, didn't he?"

I didn't answer. I'm pretty sure Dad didn't want Mr. Hotchkins to know that he told me what to write.

"How about it, son? Mr. Hotchkins is already sure your father told you what to put down."

"How come?"

"Because you wrote <u>because</u> instead of <u>cuz</u>. And you signed it <u>Charles B. Nichols, Jr.</u> Your other letters you signed <u>Yr frnd, Boomer</u>." Mr. Banks looked me in the eye. "Mr. Hotchkins is right, isn't he?"

It was no good lying. Him being a lawyer and all, I felt like I was on the witness stand. I just nodded my head. "We really do need a tractor, though."

"Well, that will be up to Mr. Hotchkins."
Then he thanked me for being honest and for
showing him around and for the coffee. I wished
him luck on the drive down the road in his
little car.

I spoze he made it all right. When Dad
finally got home, he didn't say anything about
any cars being stuck. And I didn't say anything to him about Mr. Banks being here,
either. I was just working up to it when Mom
called, like she does every Wednesday and
Sunday. She talked to me first, then Dad. He
closed the door so I couldn't hear. After a long
time, I heard him slam the receiver down and
swear. Then I was scared I'd be aggravating
him if I told him about Mr. Banks, so I didn't. I
didn't tell anybody, not even Mary Margaret.

She was in the library again today after
school. After I got on the bus, she walked up
to the high school to wait in the library
there. She says she will never ride the bus
again, in case Nick Sherman might be on it.

Thursday, January 14

This has been the best week in a long time.
Tuesday morning, when I got a ride to school
with Mr. Kreimer and Bud Willetts, Bud asked
me if I could spend the weekend after next
taking care of his dogs, Trixie and Taffy. He
and Mr. Kreimer want to go to a get-together
of their old marine buddies.

Trixie is getting ready to have puppies,
probably not until a couple of days after they
get home. But Bud is afraid she just might
have them early. And he doesn't want to
leave her out in the cold kennel for the whole

weekend, anyway.

"You can either stay in my trailer, or come down and check on her two or three times a day," he said.

"If I stay in the trailer, can I bring Sunny?"

"Sure." So that is what I'll do. Dad won't miss me. He is hardly home weekends, now. Ever since that Christmas dinner with Mom, he has been getting worse. It's a good thing we already had a freezer full of food when she left.

I told Mr. Kreimer I would be glad to feed his cows and chickens, too. I used to think he was an old grouch. He still is not exactly friendly. When I ride with him and Bud in the mornings, it's Bud that does most of the talking. But I notice that lots of times Mr. Kreimer is just coming down the drive at the right time to pick me up. I think he might even wait sometimes until he sees me coming. It will be fun to stay by myself in Bud's trailer and take care of the dogs and the animals.

But what I really want to write about is what happened later during lunch. Nick

Sherman and I were both in the boys' bath-room. He said, "How's your redheaded friend? Did she tell you about making out with me? She's sure got nice—"

"Shut your mouth, you liar!" I said before he could finish.

"What redhead?" one of the other kids asked.

"Shut your mouth," I yelled up at Nick before he could answer. "I mean it." By then I had my fist ready.

"You and who else, farmer boy?" Then he took a swing at me. I was ready for him. I ducked and came up with my right under his

78

jaw. There is one thing about living in the country and doing chores, especially now that I do chores at Dinah's, too. I'm plenty strong. But I was surprised, myself, at the crunching sound and the way Nick fell back. One of the other kids caught him or he would've landed on the floor. And blood was coming from his lip, too.

When I saw the blood, I felt real strange inside, kind of sick-like. The thing is, I wanted to get him, all right, but then right after I did, I wished that I had made myself stop. 'Course, there was no way to take it back now.

The campus supervisor walked in just as I was saying, "Why didn't you just shut your mouth like I told you?"

Then we had to go to the dean's office. The first thing he asked was, "What's this all about?"

"Nothing," I said.

"What have you got to say?" He looked at Nick. Nick's lip was already swelling.

"I told him to shut his mouth," I said before Nick could answer, and I raised my fist.

The dean didn't see it, but Nick did.

The dean looked back at me. "Why did you tell him to shut his mouth?"

"I don't want to talk about it, just like I didn't want him to talk about it."

"Well, then," the dean said, looking back and forth at us, "who hit whom first?"

"He did," Nick said. "I never even touched him."

"Is that right, Charles?" the dean asked.

"He swung and he missed. Left himself wide open. I got him a good one under the jaw."

There was some more, but it wound up with Nick having to write "I will not provoke a fight" one hundred times. He had to bring it in the next day. The dean said I was lucky I'd never been in trouble before. I only had to go to detention one day and write "I will not strike another student" one hundred times. I was spozed to go after school Wednesday, but I told the dean I had to help Dinah that day, so he let me go today instead.

I thought I would have to take the late bus home after detention and walk home in the dark. But when I told Mary Margaret all that happened, she asked her mother to please give me a ride all the way home.

Mary Margaret says Nick Sherman didn't get detention because his father is on the school board. But her mother says it's probably because Nick didn't actually hit me. I don't care. At least maybe he has learned to keep his big mouth shut. It's not fair for rats like him to talk that way about nice girls like Mary Margaret.

On the way home in the car, her mother asked me if I'd like to go to the play Patrick is in tomorrow night. "Would your parents mind if you came home from school with us and had dinner? We'll go to the play from there."

"They won't care," I said.

"Well, be sure to ask."

"I will, as soon as my dad gets home," I said. If he doesn't come home tonight, I'll just leave him a note. He won't care, anyway. I called Dinah to tell her I'd help her early Saturday morning instead of tomorrow afternoon.

I've never been to a play before. And I'm kind of scared about meeting Mary Margaret's dad—after she told me what he would do if he ever found out about Nick Sherman. I bet he's pretty strict about Mary Margaret. I hope he likes me all right.

Saturday, January 16

After we picked up Patrick at the high school, Mary Margaret's mother stopped at The Tamale Factory and bought some tamales to take out. When we got to their house, Mary Margaret helped her mother get the dinner ready. Patrick asked me to help him feed Tinker and the other horses. I think Tinker remembered me cuz he neighed when he saw me.

Their house is not one of the big expensive new ones. Patrick says it was there a long time before all the new houses. It's still a nice house, but you can tell it is old, just like mine.

Patrick acted funny, like he had something on his mind. I thought he was nervous because of being in the play that night. But finally he said, "I've been wantin' to tell you thanks for what you did to that Nick Sherman."

"Who told you?"

"Mary Margaret."

"What'd she tell you?"

"That he'd been makin' nasty remarks about her in the boys' bathroom. You told him to shut his mouth. Then you socked him and shut it for him."

I figured from that, that Mary Margaret hadn't told him what Nick had done to her that time after school, just that he was mouthing off about her. "I got him good," I told him. "Right in the jaw. His lip was bleeding." I was bragging to Patrick, but really I was feeling kind of bad about it. While I was in the detention room, Mr. Coburn gave me a good talking to about violence not being the right answer. He says somebody as smart as me should use his brains, not his fists.

"He's a pain. His own sister says so. She

sits by me in a couple of classes," Patrick said.

"Did she say anything about the fight?"

"She didn't know about it until I told her. Nick's lip was all swollen up that night. Natalie says he told his folks that someone on the bus pushed him and he fell. He's been gettin' his mother to pick him up ever since."

"Suits me fine if he <u>never</u> rides the bus again," I said.

About then, Mary Margaret's father drove up. Patrick told him I was Mary Margaret's friend who lived over in Freel Canyon.

He shook my hand and said, "Call me Murph. Everybody else does."

"Most people call me Boomer," I told him.

"Boomer," he said, smiling. "Sounds like a good name for a marine. Matter of fact there's a general they call Boomer. General Boomer Kilborn."

Mary Margaret's father is a sergeant in the marines, and in his uniform, it didn't seem right for me to call him just "Murph," but I noticed that everybody else does, even

Mary Margaret. Mostly I said "sir."

We had the tamales and some enchiladas for dinner. Mary Margaret's mother is Mexican and she made the enchiladas herself.

They sure were good. She says she can make tamales, too, but it is so much work, she doesn't have time. She says the ones from The Tamale Factory are just as good. Boy, <u>are</u> they good! I ate three and an enchilada and salad besides.

We ate in the kitchen at a big round table. At first I was nervous. I was a little afraid of Mary Margaret's father. But everybody was very friendly.

Murph wanted to know what I like in school and if I am going out for any sports. I told

him I can't because I live so far from school
and don't have transportation. Mary Margaret
told him I'm learning to ride her horse and
that I'm already plenty strong. She looked at
me when she said that. I knew she was thinking of how I socked Nick Sherman.

Murph says he has some weight training
equipment I can borrow. He wants me to
think about joining the marines when I get
out of school. I told him about Mr. Kreimer
and Bud Willetts going to their marine get-
together next weekend and how I'm going to
take care of their place for them.

After dinner, I put on my new Western
shirt I got from Mom for Christmas. It was
still in the box. I took it to school that morning so I'd have it to change into for the play.

The play was funny and we all laughed a
lot. A couple of people forgot their words, but
Patrick did all of his just right. Afterward we
went to the Yummie Donut Shoppe. Mrs.
Murphy was afraid my folks would worry. I
told her Mom didn't live with us anymore and
that Dad knew I'd be out late.

When we got to my house, it was dark. I figured Dad wasn't even home yet, but I told the Murphys I guessed he was probably in bed. I didn't want them to worry. I'm used to being home alone.

Seems like Dad is gone most of the time. He's had three long distance calls this last week, when he wasn't home. One was early in the morning after he'd already gone to work. The other times were at night. I told the operator he was at work and I didn't know when he'd be home. I could hear a man's voice on the other end kind of snorting.

I wonder if it is Mr. Hotchkins or Mr. Banks calling. Dad has been waiting to get an answer about the tractor. I never did tell him about Mr. Banks coming here. I wish I'd told him right away, even if he was in a bad mood. Now that I've put off telling him so long, it seems too late.

Mary Margaret rode Tinker over this morning and gave me another riding lesson. Afterward I packed sandwiches and we took Sunny for a hike up the canyon for lunch.

Mostly we just talked. I never thought a girl could be so easy to talk to. When it was time to start back, I kissed her again. She said it made her feel good. It made me feel good, too.

When we got back, Dad was working in the barn, so Mary Margaret finally got to meet him. He was polite and talked to her about her horse and how they train them for the studios. He was in a good mood. I hope it lasts.

Saturday, January 23

Here I am in Bud Willetts's trailer. I just
ate some of the spaghetti and meatballs
Bud left for me. He's a good cook. Trixie is
just fine. She and Sunny and Taffy are getting
along okay now that Trixie has made sure
Sunny knows that Trixie is the boss dog. I
have to keep them all in the trailer because
it's been raining since early this afternoon.

Mary Margaret and Patrick rode over
this morning. Patrick said Mr. Kreimer's place
reminds him of Ireland, especially since there's
been so much rain. He walked around and

looked at the cows and stuff while Mary Margaret and I rode up in the canyon. I was on Tinker and she was on Patrick's horse, Silver Belle. I looked around for Dutch, but it's probably just as well I didn't see him. Most likely, the coyotes didn't leave much.

I like riding horses better when there is some place to go and somebody to ride with. I'd still rather have a motorcycle than a horse, though. Any day. I'm pretty sure I'll have enough money by this summer.

Mr. Kreimer and Bud said they are going to pay me for this weekend. I'm not going to take it though. Mr. Kreimer gives me a ride to school every day. If it's raining, he takes me all the way instead of just to the Alpha-Beta.

When it's raining, Dinah brings me home from the bus stop on the afternoons I work for her. Lots of times she and I have dinner together. Slim doesn't get home until after seven. Now that the baby is growing in her, she says she gets too hungry to wait until then. Now she eats dinner with me instead and then she eats dessert with him.

Slim is going on location next week. Dinah's going with him, for almost two weeks. I'm going to take care of her chickens for her while she's away.

My muscles are getting bigger and stronger all the time. I used to put only nine or ten shovels of chicken feed in the wheelbarrow. Now I put in thirteen. And I  can lift a whole 100-pound sack of chicken feed all by myself. I'm a lot stronger than that Nick Sherman, even if I am shorter. And I'm not so short now, either. With my boots, Mary Margaret and I are even, so I'm catching up to her.

Dad says I shouldn't worry about being short. He says boys get taller later than girls. He's almost six feet and my real mom was five feet, nine inches, he says, so I will be on the tall side almost for sure.

Dad never talked about my real mom before.

But last week, he got out some pictures of her. She was pretty. He has a picture of her holding me when I was just a tiny baby. And there was a picture of her and him and me when he was holding me. He said I could have the pictures to keep.

I wanted to ask him about the accident. I wasn't even one year old when she was killed. But I was scared I would be aggravating him. One day when I was cleaning up the house, I found a box of papers under his chest of drawers. It was mostly letters from Grandma and some forms. It looked like Dad went to jail after the accident, and Grandma didn't want to let him have me after he got out. Then there was something about a custody decision with some papers signed by a judge. I never told Dad I found the papers.

When he was showing me the pictures, he put his arm around me. "You're all I've got now, Boomer," he said. "I'm sorry if I'm rough on you sometimes."

"That's okay. I understand."

"How about we go out for dinner tomorrow

night? What restaurant shall we go to?"

"How about The Tamale Factory? They have good tamales. Mary Margaret's mother got some to take out that day I was over there."

That was Tuesday night. But on Wednesday he didn't show up until almost nine o'clock. He said he'd had to work late and we could go some other time. But I could smell booze on his breath. I think he stopped at a bar on the way home. But mostly he has been pretty good. I haven't seen any whiskey bottles around all week.

Dad is so nice sometimes. I wish he was like that all the time. I don't need him to take me to restaurants, if only I didn't have to worry what he will do when he is drunk.

He still hasn't heard from Mr. Hotchkins. I'm sort of worried what Mr. Hotchkins will decide about the tractor. Bud Willetts has a bunch of Louis L'Amour books. They're all about cowboys and pioneers and stuff. I'm already halfway through one, so I'm going to crawl in bed and read until I get sleepy—if the rain will let me go to sleep. It's coming down real hard tonight. In this trailer, it sounds even worse.

I hope Mr. Coburn is right when he says writing about things that bother you can make you feel better.

Mr. Kreimer and Bud didn't get home until late last night. Bud loaned me some of his Louis L'Amour books and gave me a ride home.

I changed into my pajamas and was fixing myself some hot cocoa when Dad came out of his room. He was really drunk. He'd probably been drinking since he got the mail Saturday afternoon.

"Who the hell is this Banks character?" he yelled. He waved a letter at me. The top of it looked like the paper that Mr. Hotchkins uses when he sends me the $5.00 every month.

"He's a friend of Mr. Hotchkins. He came to see me a couple weeks ago."

"You danged little sneak. You never said a word. What'd you tell him, anyway?" Dad grabbed the front of my pajamas and jerked me so hard my teeth banged.

I was feeling a little scared so I answered quickly, "Just what he asked me. Where Mom is, when you get home from work, what I like best in school. All kinds of things."

"You sure did tell him <u>all kinds of things.</u> What'd you tell him about the tractor—that I ruined it because I forgot to put in oil?" He slapped me on the ear, hard. I couldn't duck because he still had me by my pajama top.

"I never did. I told him it ran out of oil and got ruined. I didn't say anything about you."

He smacked me again, harder. "You liar. Listen to this." He read something from the letter, about how my grandmother did not intend for the money to be used to replace equipment that my dad ruined through his own carelessness.

"I didn't say anything about carelessness. I said it ran out of oil. I told him I thought we should have a big tractor so I could learn on it." I was really frightened by this time, and my ear was ringing from the blows. Dad didn't seem to believe what I was telling him.

"But you didn't say a word about how it would help you get a job at the studios, did you?"

"I did. He asked me. I told him working for the studios would be okay with me."

"Then what's all this about Mr. Banks reporting you have the interest and potential to go into anthropology and you ought to go to college?" He was reading from the letter when he said that. "You lying little sneak," he yelled. He lurched at me and shoved me against the stove.

Suddenly I felt an awful pain in my back. My pajamas were on fire! I pushed passed Dad and raced to the shower. I kept the water on long enough to get the fire out. I locked the door and looked at my back in the mirror. It had shriveled-up black stuff all over. It must have been what was left of the pajamas. It made me sick to my stomach to look at it. And it hurt something awful.

I hurried back under the cold water. When I looked in the mirror again, the black stuff was gone, but my back still hurt. The only thing that helped was the cold water even if it did make me shiver. I could hear Dad crying outside the door, telling me he was sorry and how I was the only one that mattered to him. I was crying, too. I didn't answer him.

I filled the tub and flopped down on my belly and just stayed there. It was after midnight when I finally felt like I could stand being out of the water. I had to climb over Dad to get to my room. He must have passed out while I was in the tub.

He got up early and went to work. I was so sore I didn't go to school today. Besides, the left side of my face is swollen and red where Dad hit me. I stayed in bed until after he left. Then I called Mr. Kreimer and told

him not to look for me today because I was
sick. I found some burn ointment for my
back, but it doesn't help much.

It's almost dinnertime now. I feel a lot better than I did, so I guess I can go to school
tomorrow. I'll tell people I fell and hit my
head.

I went over to feed Dinah's chickens a
little while ago. It is beautiful out today. How
can the world look so nice when some of the
things that happen in it are so rotten?

When I came back from Dinah's, I managed
to put some more wood in the barn so it will
dry out. Dad used up all the dry wood I had in

there before. If he's late tonight, I'm going to
leave him a note to be sure to order more
propane. The tank is getting low and the TV
says there is a big storm coming up from off
the coast of Mexico. It's spozed to be here

Thursday night or Friday. If we run out of propane we won't have any heat except the fireplace and no way to cook on the stove, either.

Mary Margaret called me while I was writing this. She wanted to know if I was sick. I told her I fell and hit my head and had a headache. I don't want her to know what happened.

Mr. Coburn is right. Now that I've written it all down, I feel better. I think putting it on paper helped as much as the cold bath. For a while I didn't even feel like eating. But now I think I will go finish the rest of the spaghetti Bud Willetts gave me—while we still have gas to heat it. It's good spaghetti, but I don't know how good it would be cold.

I sure hope the propane gets here before the storm comes.

Saturday, January 30

   The weatherman was right. We did have a
big storm Thursday night, just like he said we
would. And sure enough we ran out of propane,
just like I was afraid we would.
   It wasn't Dad's fault. On Monday and
Tuesday and Wednesday he was as nice as
he can be, when he feels like it and isn't drinking. I told him Monday night about the propane
gas being low. He called them on Tuesday, but
he had to go in and pay ahead before they
would deliver. On Wednesday he went in and
paid, but the lady said the earliest they

could get out to our canyon would be Friday.

Dad told them by Friday it might be too late. If the storm came our road might wash out. Even if it didn't, the people around here don't like to have heavy trucks on the road when the ground is soaked. He told her those big tires sink in so far they make big ruts. The water can't get out of such deep ruts and the road turns to muck. Dad said it was like talking to a brick wall. Friday was the earliest they could come, she said, but they would try for Friday morning.

Sure enough, just like the TV said, on Thursday afternoon it started to pour while I was over taking care of Dinah's chickens. By the time I was ready to come home, our road was flooded. The ground was already soaked from the last rains. Water came rushing down the canyon walls like it was coming out of fire hoses.

The road had turned into a river. I took off my shoes and rolled up my pants and waded. The water was rushing so fast it was hard to keep my balance. Rocks as big as a man's

head tumbled past. My ankles are all black and blue from where smaller rocks I couldn't see banged into me. And cold! That water felt like ice. I was still shivering after I got in the house.

And, sure enough, the heater had gone out. We'd run out of gas. I piled wood in the fireplace and got a good fire going. Then I took a shower with the water that was still warm in the tank.

I knew the road would be even worse farther down the canyon, so I didn't expect Dad to even try it. I figured he might call me, but when I checked the phone, it was dead. I just hoped the water wouldn't get too high while I was home all by myself.

I put on Dad's big poncho and brought in all the wood from the barn. Then I put some more in the barn to start drying out. Even with the poncho, I had to change into dry clothes again. For dinner I cooked hot dogs in the fireplace. I heated water in the electric coffee maker to make cocoa and some soup from a package.

I slept in the living room in front of the fireplace. I was so pooped out I never even heard all the rain that must have come down in the night. When I got up in the morning, there was water everywhere. It hadn't come into the house yet, but the ditch me and Dad dug had turned into a big wash. There was almost a foot of water in the barn. When I saw that, I finally got pretty worried. All the wood I had put in there to dry was sopping wet.

I put on Dad's rubber boots so I could wade over to Dinah's to feed her chickens. There was so much water I couldn't even see where the road was spozed to be. I decided to wait until later when maybe the water wouldn't be so high. The rain seemed to be letting up a little and I knew the chickens would be okay until that afternoon.

After I got on some more dry clothes and rubbed Sunny with a towel, I made cocoa again and had some toast I made in the fire-place. I turned on the TV. They said there was flooding all over the county. It showed some pictures of houses with water right in them. At least our house didn't have any water in it. Not yet.

I almost jumped out of my chair when Sunny suddenly started barking her head off. I looked out. It was Mr. Kreimer, on Patrick's horse and leading Tinker, coming to get me. Boy, was I glad to see him. I was glad I knew how to ride Tinker, too.

We went to Dinah's first and put out enough feed and scratch for a couple of days, in case I couldn't get back. Then Mr. Kreimer took us around a back way behind Dinah's. There were lots of little washes we had to get across. It's a good thing Sunny loves the water. Most of the time she splashed across the washes by herself, but a couple of times the water was too deep and too fast. When we got to those places, Mr. Kreimer put her up on Tinker with me, then he took Tinker's reins and led him across while he rode Patrick's horse. He said it's a good thing Tinker knew me and Sunny or we might not have got away with it.

When we got to his house, Mary Margaret's father was there. I'd told Mary Margaret about our propane being low. So she'd tried to call me on the phone to see if we still had gas. When my phone was dead, she called her dad at work. He called Mr. Kreimer, who was already making plans to hike up and get me. They fixed it up that Patrick and Mary Margaret brought the horses over to Mr. Kreimer's and then went home.

I was glad, for once, that Mary Margaret wasn't there, and that it was her father who had come to take the horses back home. I'd already gone through all my good school clothes. The jeans I was wearing were full of holes and sopping wet besides. I looked terrible.

And that's not the only reason I was glad she wasn't there. I'll maybe write about that later. Right now I don't want to think about it.

Friday, February 5

I'm still here at Mr. Kreimer's. I might as well put down why. After Mr. Kreimer and I got to his place on the horses during the flood, he told me to stand by the fire. He gave me some of his clothes to change into. I put on the T-shirt and wool shirt first. They were way too big but I didn't care. I was just getting into tho big old jeans when he came back with a pair of Bud's sweat pants.

He handed them to me. "These ain't going to fit, either, but at least they'll push up or roll up better than those jeans."

"Thanks." I bent over to pull the sweat pants on.

"What in tarnation is that on your back, boy?" Before I could move away he'd pulled up the shirt and T-shirt. "Who did this to you?"

I sure didn't want to tell on Dad. But there is something about Mr. Kreimer. It was no good lying. Besides, after how he came after me in the flood, I figured I owed him the truth. So I told him what happened that Sunday night with Dad, after Bud drove me home. I told him it was an accident, that Dad didn't realize there was a burner on.

"Drunk as a skunk, I reckon," he said. He called in Bud and Mary Margaret's father. He said he wanted them as witnesses. He made me tell them both all over again.

"Has he hurt you before, Boomer?" Mary Margaret's dad asked. He turned my face to the light, looking at the black and blue mark.

"Not like this. He's licked me with his belt, and punched me. It's only when he's had too much to drink. And I guess this time he was too mad to notice if the stove was lit or not."

110

"What happened this time? What's he mad about?" Murph asked me.

So I had to explain about Dad wanting me to use some of Grandma's money for a tractor. And about Mr. Banks coming to see me and asking a lot of questions. And Mr. Hotchkins saying my dad couldn't have the money because Grandma wanted me to have it to go to college.

Bud Willetts took some pictures of my back and face. Then he and Mr. Kreimer and Murph went out in the kitchen. I couldn't hear what they were saying, but I spoze it was about me.

That night for dinner Mr. Kreimer and me and Bud had steak and beans and broccoli and applesauce. I'm not all  that crazy about broccoli but I ate it anyhow. It was good to have a hot meal that somebody else cooked.

Mr. Kreimer noticed I left the broccoli for last. He said, "If you're going to be eating here, boy, you'll be eating a lot of vegetables."

"The Alpha-Beta throws out a lot of stuff that's got enough spots on it so people won't buy it at the high prices they have to charge," Bud explained. "All you need is a sharp knife to trim it. By the time it's cooked nobody knows the difference, anyway."

I've already eaten more vegetables this week than I ate all of last year. I've been staying here at Mr. Kreimer's ever since he came and got me in the flood. We left a note for Dad to tell him where I was, but he didn't show up at Mr. Kreimer's until Sunday afternoon. I spoze he figured I was okay because I'm used to being alone. And the phone was out so he couldn't call me. He probably forgot about the propane being low.

When he showed up on Sunday, Mr. Kreimer saw him coming up the drive. He told me to stay in the house and hollered at Bud, who was out by the cows. He and Bud talked to Dad out in the driveway. I watched out the window but I couldn't hear. Dad's head was looking down, mostly. Just before he left he looked up toward the house, but I don't think he saw me in the window. He didn't wave or anything.

Mr. Kreimer said he's giving Dad a week to pull himself together. Dad's spozed to come back here this Sunday afternoon. "We'll decide then what's to be done," Mr. Kreimer said.

"By then we'll have those pictures back," Bud said.

"Sergeant Murphy said he'd be glad to come over if we need him," Mr. Kreimer added.

That got me worrying about Mary Margaret finding out what had happened. I worried about it a lot, but when I talked to her in the library this week, she didn't say anything about it. Her dad must not have told her about Dad hurting me.

She thinks I am staying at Mr. Kreimer's because of the floods. It could be, too. We had another storm come in on Wednesday. By the time I got off the bus after school, it was pouring. Bud Willetts was there in the truck to pick me up.

Thursday morning I didn't think we would make it out in Mr. Kreimer's truck. When the propane truck finally came, it churned up the road real good, just like Dad said it would. The ruts filled with water, making big mud holes. It was so gooshy in spots that a couple of times we turned almost sideways. Pretty exciting. (I wonder what that Mr. Banks would say if he could see our road now!) But by afternoon, the rain had let up and the water was draining off again.

This has sure been a wet year. Every day when I go up to Dinah's, I put out an extra lot of chicken feed and scratch, just in case I can't get back for a while. Dinah and Slim are spozed to be back from location tomorrow or Sunday.

Mary Margaret is going to come here to Mr. Kreimer's tomorrow with Tinker—if it doesn't start to rain again. Today the sun was out. The hills look so green Bud Willetts says it almost puts his eyes out. This is the first spring that he has been here. He thought our hills were always brown. He's been taking pictures of our canyon. Maybe he will take a picture of Mary Margaret for me.

I wonder what will happen Sunday when Dad comes and they show him the pictures of my back and face.

Sunday, February 7

Dad hasn't shown up yet and it is already three o'clock. I'm kind of nervous about what will happen when he comes. I hope he won't be drinking.

I tried playing with Sunny but she was more interested in hanging around Bud's trailer. Now that Trixie's puppies have their eyes open, they are cute. Bud has them in his trailer in a big box. Sunny can hear them and smell them from outside. She keeps hanging around the door to the trailer, wanting to go in. Bud says maybe that means she'll be a good mother herself someday.

I tried reading a book, too, but I can't keep my mind on it, so I'm trying to write instead. My room here at Mr. Kreimer's isn't very big. It has a bed and this table I'm writing on and a closet with built-in drawers for clothes. It used to be Mr. Kreimer's wife's sewing room. Bud told me Mr. Kreimer's wife died a few years ago. He had a son, too, but he died in the war. I never knew he had a son. I wonder if Dinah and Slim know.

They got home yesterday. This morning Dinah stopped by to pay me. I didn't want to take any money, but she said it was worth it. She'd heard about our flood on the TV, but she said she didn't worry about the chickens because I was taking care of them.

Mary Margaret came over yesterday morning. She was on Silver Belle and leading Tinker. We took a long ride up the canyon behind Mr. Kreimer's. It's real pretty now, with lots of little streams and new springs seeping right out of the hills.

I wish the springs would last until summer

when it's so hot and dry here. Mr. Kreimer says there will be a lot of jacks and cotton-tails and ground squirrels this year because of all the rain making food for little animals. He says he'll take me hunting.

Mary Margaret and I stopped under a big oak tree and turned the horses loose. Green grass is already coming up for them to munch on. We watched them and at first we talked about what a beautiful day it was. But then she said, "I'm kind of surprised you're still at Mr. Kreimer's. Didn't the propane truck come?"

"Yeah, it came. Chewed up the road pretty bad," I said.

"Can't you get up to your house? Is the road washed out?"

"It's okay. I went up to get my clothes last week."

"Well, so how come you're still living at Mr. Kreimer's?"

I didn't answer her for a while. I picked up a rock and pretended I was looking at it. "There could be gold here," I told her. "My mom found a flake of it once, right up in the canyon behind us."

"Are you going to keep on living at Mr. Kreimer's?" When Mary Margaret wants to know something, she doesn't give up easy.

"It's something I don't want to talk about, kind of a secret."

"But Charlie, aren't we friends? I told you my secret about what happened with that awful Nick Sherman. And you made me feel a lot better about it, too."

"It's just something I don't want to talk about."

"Well, if that's the way you're going to be, we might as well go back." She whistled for the horses.

So then I had to tell her. Besides Sunny and my friend Jake, she's the best friend I have in the whole world. I never thought I would have a girl for a best friend.

It wasn't so bad. She made me show her my back. It is getting a lot better. She said I should never ever go back and live with my dad. If Mr. Kreimer doesn't want me, she said she will ask her folks if I can live with them.

She said her dad and mom both like me and so does Patrick.

"And I like you a whole lot, Charlie," she said. I put my arm around her and she leaned her head on my shoulder. I like Mary Margaret's family a lot, too. But I like her so much, it might not be a good idea for me to live in the same house with her. She took the rubber band off her ponytail so her hair was loose and I could run my hand through it.

We might've sat there a long time, but she had to get back with the horses so Patrick and his girlfriend could go riding with some kids in Stone Canyon. On the way back I rode Silver Belle instead of Tinker. She's higher than Tinker, over sixteen hands. What a funny way to measure horses. Mary Margaret warned me not to let Silver Belle take me under a tree. She likes to go under the low branches and make her rider duck way down.

When we got back, Mr. Kreimer said Mom had called. So after Mary Margaret left, I called her back. I don't know how much Mr. Kreimer has told her. Probably the whole thing.

She didn't say anything about it, but she said she might come out this afternoon, too.

There is a motorcycle coming up the driveway now. Sunny is barking her head off. My gosh, it's Mom! I didn't even know she could ride a motorcycle!

Friday, February 12

Last Sunday, while me and Bud were looking at Mom's motorcycle, she and Mr. Kreimer
went off a ways from us to talk. Then when
Dad showed up, Mr. Kreimer said he wanted
everyone to come in the house.

Mom said, "Maybe you should wait out
here, Boomer."

"He better come, too," Mr. Kreimer said.
"Come on, boy. We gotta discuss what's best
for you. You're old enough to have a say in it."
He opened the kitchen door and pointed at
the table for us to all sit down.

Before he even sat down, Dad said, "I don't know why <u>you</u> should have any say in it, Jed." He glared at Bud. "And what in the blue blazes are you doing here?"

"Bud's a witness," Mr. Kreimer said.

"Have all the witnesses you want. Boomer's my son, nobody else's. You're just trying to make trouble, Jed. You got a grudge against me, ever since I called the county and they made you fence in your cows."

"What I'm trying to do is keep the county out of it this time, Chuck. If I call the county and tell them how you been treating this boy, they'll snatch him away and put him in a foster home."

"What do you mean, how I been treating him?"

"Hitting him, pushing him against a lighted burner, that's what I mean," Mr. Kreimer said. Bud shoved the pictures of my back and face at Dad.

"Can I help it if the kid fell on the stove and his pajamas caught fire?" Dad looked at me when he said it. "How about it, Boomer, ain't that what happened?"

I looked down at my hand, and rubbed on a little scratch I had there. I was afraid if I said the truth, later on, when Dad was drunk, he'd beat me again for it.

"You got him too scared to speak up for himself, Chuck Nichols," Mom said. "But we all know who put those burns and bruises on the boy."

"Who's gonna believe you when the boy hisself ain't talking?" Dad said.

"Why you no-good bully," Mr. Kreimer said. He stood up and grabbed the front of Dad's shirt.

"Hey, hey," said Bud. "Let go, Jed. That isn't going to help. Sit down." He tugged at Mr. Kreimer's sleeve until he sat down.

"The beating and burning isn't the only thing, Mr. Nichols," Bud said. "There's the boy, and Jed and me <u>and</u> a marine sergeant who can swear you left Boomer alone in an unheated house during the flood. Didn't even try to get in to help him until two days later."

"And I got a telephone bill to show how

many times I called on a Wednesday or Sunday evening," Mom said. "How many of those nights were you home, Chuck, in all these weeks I've called? Maybe half. Maybe not even that," Mom said.

"Can I help it if I gotta work late?"

"Hunh! You're forgetting I know what bars you hang out in. Plenty of witnesses there, too. Don't give me that stuff about always working late," she told him.

Dad glared at her. "Well, what are you going to do about it?"

"We're going to figure out something else for the boy. That's what we're going to do," Mr. Kreimer said.

"He'd better come along with me," Mom said. "Irene's other roommate moved out. There's plenty of room."

So then we had an argument. I said I didn't want to because I couldn't take Sunny. And I didn't want to have to start in a different school. I was thinking mostly of Sunny and Mary Margaret. But I didn't want to go to a new school, either. I like Mr. Coburn and my

P. E. teacher. Except for the jerks from Stone Canyon like Nick Sherman, there's some nice guys that are a lot of fun, too. I sure didn't want to start all over in a new school not knowing anybody.

Then Dad said, "Why don't you come home with me, Boomer? I never meant to hurt you like that. It won't happen again, I promise."

"Promises, promises!" Mom said.

"What about it, Boomer?" Mr. Kreimer asked me. "You want to go back with your dad or you want to stay on here for a while?"

It was awful. I know that inside Dad loves me. He had that big fight to get me away from Grandma. And now he wanted me to come home with him. He was dead sober and looking at me with an awful pleading look in his eyes.

But his eyes were bloodshot. I remembered the times he'd hit Mom, the times he'd hit me and shook me, and the awful burn I got from the stove. It seemed like every time he'd gotten mad it had gotten a little worse. What would happen the next time he got drunk?

"I don't want to go back unless I know you ain't gonna drink anymore. I'll stay here. I can pay Mr. Kreimer the $50 from Grandma every month. And I can work for him, too."

"I'll quit," Dad said. "Right now. I'll never touch whiskey or hard liquor again."

"I've heard that before and so has Boomer," Mom said. "Talk is cheap. You're going to have to do better than just talk about it for the boy to believe you."

Mr. Kreimer said he'd be glad to have me, but he thought it was only right that Dad pay for my keep. So they fixed it up that Dad is going to come by every Sunday morning and pay Mr. Kreimer $50. And if Dad is sober, I'm going to spend Sunday with him. And if everything goes all right, then after a while I can spend the whole weekend with him.

The weekends are the worst times for Dad. I hope this time ho means it when he says he will quit drinking. Mr. Kreimer says if Dad ever lays a hand on me again, he, Mr. Kreimer, will take it out of Dad's hide.

After Dad left, Mom took me for a ride on her motorcycle. We went up to our house to get my helmet. Mom thanked Dad for giving it to me for Christmas. She knows a kid who was riding without a helmet when a car pulled right in front of him. It wasn't his fault or anything. But now his brain is all messed up. Mom said he is like a kindergartner. He even wets his pants sometimes.

Mom took me all the way up Stone Canyon and back. When we got home, she and Dad talked for a while. He wanted her to come out and be at our house on Sunday, too. She said she couldn't this Sunday, but maybe next time. I hope so. When she called Wednesday night she said she hoped so, too.

Dad called a little while ago. He sounded sober. We are spozed to go to The Tamale Factory on Sunday. I hope we make it this time.

Monday, February 22

The reason I didn't write much here lately is because I been busy. Mr. Kreimer started getting a lot of milk and cottage cheese from the dairy man at the Alpha-Beta. Once it goes past the date on the carton, they can't sell it. Mr. Kreimer said it was a shame to throw it out, but his cows don't want it.

So Saturday before last Mr. Kreimer and Bud and I went to an auction, up in Lancaster. We bought a couple of little pigs and put them in a pen Mr. Kreimer had from when he had pigs before. Mary Margaret thinks they are real cute, so she and I are going to raise

them for 4-H. Her folks paid Mr. Kreimer for one, and I paid for the other one. They are both going to stay here at Mr. Kreimer's. Besides the things from the Alpha-Beta, we feed them grain.

On Saturdays Mary Margaret rides over on Tinker and we clean out their pen. Then we ride Tinker down to Katie Hart's house. Mrs. Hart is our 4-H leader. Mary Margaret is worrying about what will happen when the pigs are big enough and have to be butchered. Mrs. Hart says by the time they are that big, they'll be such a pain we'll be glad to get rid of them.

On Monday and Wednesday and Friday afternoons, I work at Dinah's. On Tuesday and Thursday, Mary Margaret rides the bus with me to the mailboxes and we walk to Mr. Kreimer's house and feed the pigs together and stuff. Then she goes home over the hill, the back way. I usually walk her part way.

Besides that, I am going to meetings for kids whose folks drink too much. It is run by the Alcoholics Anonymous people. I go with Bud every Saturday at 5:00. Bud says he has been in A. A. for eight years. Mr. Kreimer usually has a beer for dinner, but Bud always has orange pop or milk. He drinks a lot of coffee, too.

Dad still drinks beer, but I think he is keeping his promise not to touch whiskey again. Bud has talked to him about going to A. A. meetings with him, but Dad says he won't have any problems with drinking anymore. He will just stick to beer.

I don't know if we are getting along better because he's not drinking so much anymore, or maybe it's because we are only together on Sundays. Anyway, he has been real nice to me again. I just hope it lasts this time. It never did before.

Saturday, February 27

I've been pretty busy this week. Monday night, Bud's other dog, Taffy, had her puppies. She was wanting to go in and out of his trailer all day, Bud said, like she couldn't make up her mind what she wanted.

Then, while Mr. Kreimer and I were eating dinner, Bud came over and said to hurry up and finish eating. Taffy was in her bed, he said, getting ready to have her pups. So Mr. Kreimer and I both went over. I never saw anything getting born before.

When we got there, Taffy kept switching

around. First she'd lie down with her head pointed one way. Then she'd get up and turn around. Bud patted her and told her what a good dog she was, and finally she calmed down and stretched out. Then pretty quick she stuck her nose back under her tail and I saw a little dark lump come out of her.

Taffy licked and licked at it until I could see it was a little wet puppy. By the time she got through licking, it was looking almost dry, kind of a soft brown color. A few minutes later, Taffy gave another push and pretty soon she had another pup to take care of.

Altogether she had eight puppies. Bud says she has had as many as eleven, but eight is better. Then she has room for them to all eat at once.

But what has been keeping me busy is that one of the puppies is a real little runt. She is wiggly and strong, but too little to make it on her own, Bud says. The other big puppies push and shove to get at Taffy's faucets, and the little one has a hard time getting her share. So Bud and I feed her with a bottle. Bud has a special kind of powder that he mixes with warm water. He puts it in a little bottle like girls play dolls with. It works real good.

Bud still keeps the little one with Taffy so she gets some of Taffy's milk, too, and so Taffy can lick her and keep her clean and take care of her. Bud says it is important that the mother dog lick the puppy. He says everybody needs to be loved, even puppies.

In the morning, when Taffy has lots of milk, Bud puts the runt on one of the best faucets and keeps the other puppies from pushing her off. He helps her again around lunchtime. Then when I get home from school, I give her a bottle, and after dinner I give her another one. Bud says I don't have to, that he can do it. But I like to do it. I call the runt "Spunky." When I'm holding the bottle for her, she pushes with her paws, just like my hand was her mother.

When she gets through with the bottle, I hold her up under my chin and she kind of nuzzles around. I sit in Bud's big rocking chair and rock with her. She is so soft and warm.

Bud says it will be a while before we know if she is going to make it. He said, "Don't get too attached to her. She is spunky all right, but anything can happen with such a little one." He keeps a heating pad under one end of Taffy's bed. When Taffy is gone, the puppies sleep on the warm heating pad. I sure hope nothing goes wrong. I never knew little puppies could be like Spunky. I feel like I just want to hold her up under my neck and love her all the time.

Tuesday, March 16

For once it's a good thing I'm left-handed, now that I broke my other arm. It's all because I was showing off for Mary Margaret. I was walking her home after we fed the pigs. We tried a short cut from Mr. Kreimer's to her house, instead of the way we usually go. We came to a dropoff where we had to jump down.

Mary Margaret said we should turn around and go the regular way. It did look pretty far down. But I told her I'd jump, then reach up and help her get down. When I jumped, my foot slipped. I lost my balance and landed on my hand, hard. I knew right off my arm was broken.

Mary Margaret got down on her hands and knees and kind of slid down to me. She helped me back to Mr. Kreimer's and he took me to the doctor's. The cast comes way up over my elbow. I hate it. I can still feed the pigs, but Mary Margaret cleans the pens by herself. Bud is taking care of Dinah's chores for her.

Then, the Sunday after it happened, Mom came up on her motorcycle. She picked me up at Mr. Kreimer's and took me to our house on the motorcycle. She let Dad take me for a ride on it. We went up in the canyon and then down on the paved road. We were just past the Harts' house when we wiped out. I think Dad was showing off and we were traveling too fast. The first thing I knew I was on the ground. Dad was on the ground next to me.

He was knocked out at first. I had my helmet on and my head was okay. The cast was real messed up but it didn't break. My shoulder and back on that side hurt pretty bad.

We don't know yet what is going to happen with Dad, but there is going to be trouble. Katie Hart saw us when it happened. She called 911 and Mr. Kreimer. The paramedics and the sheriff and Highway Patrol all came. By the time they got there, Dad was awake again. He kept saying he was okay, just a few scratches. They took us both to the hospital, anyhow, and did a blood test on him. Turned out later, it was just below the legal limit for alcohol. But because of the accident and because he didn't have a license to ride a motorcycle, he is going to have to go to court.

Mom is mad at Dad all over again. I don't know if we will ever all get together again or not. It's okay here at Mr. Kreimer's, but it is not the same as being home. I'll be glad when Jake comes this summer. I wrote and told him if he comes as soon as school is out, he'll be here in time to watch when we butcher the pigs.

I told Katie Hart that Jake is coming from Michigan this summer. She's nice and almost as pretty as Mary Margaret. But she's too shy. Her family just moved here a couple of months ago. I feel sorry for her. I don't think she has many friends, and I know how that feels. Maybe me and Jake can take Mary Margaret and Katie to the water slide or something when it's hot this next summer.

Katie raises rabbits for 4-H, great big white ones. She walked up to Mr. Kreimer's with me and Mary Margaret one day to see our pigs. She says she thinks she'll stick to rabbits.

Thursday, April 22

Mr. Coburn was real surprised that I was already into my second notebook for this journal. I guess I have already written enough. But there is a lot to catch up on so I'll write it down anyway.

Spunky is sure doing great. She is still littler than the other puppies, but she is fat and full of fun. We are feeding the puppies baby oatmeal and scrambled eggs from Mr. Kreimer's chickens. They are all growing so fast, and getting real cute. Trixie's big puppies are nice, too, but I like Taffy's little ones better, especially Spunky.

Bud is giving Spunky to me, and I'm going to give her to Mary Margaret for her birthday for a surprise. I already asked her mother if it would be okay. Mary Margaret's birthday is on Flag Day, in June, so I will have Spunky all housebroken for her by then.

I'm sure glad I'm here at Mr. Kreimer's instead of in a foster home. I was lucky the way it worked out after the accident. When Katie called Mr. Kreimer, he and Bud came right away. Mr. Kreimer was yelling at Dad before he even got out of his truck. He was really mad. "What have you done to the boy NOW, Chuck?" he hollered.

The paramedic said he thought I might just be shook up, but they'd have to check me in the hospital. The sheriff walked over to us.

Mr. Kreimer asked where they were taking me. The sheriff wouldn't tell him. He wanted to know if Mr Kreimer was a relative. When Mr. Kreimer said no, but I was living with him, right away the sheriff wanted to know why I was living with him.

"To protect him from his drunken father." Mr. Kreimer glared at Dad.

"What do you mean?" the sheriff said.

"Just what I said. And now look what he's done. Drunk again, or I miss my guess," Mr. Kreimer said.

"It was an accident," I said. "He didn't mean to."

"Didn't mean to kill your mother, either. But he did," Mr. Kreimer said. Then he looked away, like he was sorry he'd said that.

So then the sheriff was really interested. He started writing in his book. I didn't hear just what he and Mr. Kreimer said because they walked off a little ways, but I think it was about Dad hurting me and me getting burned. They were still talking when the ambulance men loaded me up and took me to the hospital. The sheriff must have told Mr. Kreimer where I was, after all, because he showed up to visit me later that afternoon. They kept me at the hospital until the next afternoon. For observation, the doctor said.

The next morning, a lady named Blanca

came to see me in the hospital. She said she was from Children's Services. She asked a lot of questions about Dad and Mom and Mr. Kreimer, and what I ate at Mr. Kreimer's and where I slept, and about who bought my clothes, and then back to Dad and how I burned my back. When she left, she gave me a card with her name and phone number on it. I'd been thinking she worked for the hospital, but on the card it said she was from the county.

I found out later she went to see Mr. Kreimer and called Mom, too. After he'd talked that way to the sheriff about Dad, Mr. Kreimer said he was scared I'd wind up in a foster home. So after he came to see me at the hospital that afternoon, he went home and he and Bud worked their tails off cleaning house that night. Early Monday morning, they cleaned up the yard. So when Blanca came to see Mr. Kreimer, everything looked shiny clean. Bud even had all my clothes folded neat in the drawers.

Blanca and Mr. Kreimer must have got

along pretty good. He showed her my room and Sunny and Spunky and the pigs. And they had some coffee and some cake Bud had made special. So Blanca said she thought here at Mr. Kreimer's is a good place for me for a while. She said she would get the court to approve it but Mr. Kreimer would have to go see the judge. So he did.

She's been coming every week and Bud always has a cake or pie. Or sometimes Mr. Kreimer makes doughnuts. So it's working

out okay and maybe, after a while, I might go home again. But we have to wait and see what happens when Dad goes to court.

Dinah gave me a ride home from the bus

stop today. She is sure big. I wonder how babies can get born. They showed us all those pictures in Health class, but I still don't see how a baby can get out. With puppies, there's a lot of little ones, but with people it's one big one. Taffy just popped them out one at a time, easy-like. Bud says I shouldn't worry about it, that all the people in the world had to get born from women. I guess he is right and I should stop worrying about Dinah. But it still doesn't seem possible.

I will sure be glad when I get this cast off. It's a short one now, and a lot better than the one that came up over my elbow. I can reach all the way down under this one with a pencil so I can scratch where it itches. And I can do almost everything with it, but it is still a dang nuisance.

There aren't many pages left now, so I'm only going to write in the journal once in a while and maybe it will last until school is out.

Wednesday, May 5

There are only two good things about having to wear a cast on your arm. Getting it off and finding out how many friends you have.

Every Saturday Mary Margaret cleaned our pigs' pen all by herself. Mr. Kreimer helped me feed the pigs almost every day. And Bud has been doing my chores for Dinah. Even though it's out of the cast, the doctor says it will be a while before my arm is strong again, so Bud says he will do Dinah's wheelbarrowing and stuff until Jake gets here.

Dinah really needs someone to help. The

baby is going to come the end of this month, and Dinah is so big she can hardly fit behind the steering wheel. She says she is not always sure that her socks match because she can't see them. It's a good thing Bud is taking over for me.

Katie Hart is extra nice to me, too. She gets on the bus with me in the morning and we usually sit together, now that she knows me from 4-H and the accident. She doesn't think much of the Stone Canyon kids, either. (Except Mary Margaret. She likes her.) Katie's locker is near mine and we have three classes together. While my arm was in the cast, she carried books for me and helped me get my jacket on and off and things like that lots of times.

Everybody wanted to sign my cast. Even Nick Sherman. When I got the long cast off and they put on a short one,

Nick asked if he could sign that one, too. And Blanca and her friend, Mr. Harris, drew funny pictures on it.

Blanca brought him over one day after school. She said he would like to listen while we went over what had happened with me and Dad. So then Blanca asked me questions and I wound up telling the whole story over again, about Dad hurting me, and me getting burned, and Mr. Kreimer coming for me in the flood, and me deciding to stay with Mr. Kreimer until we were sure Dad was quitting drinking. I even told them about the meetings at A. A. for teenagers that I go to with Bud.

Mr. Harris kept nodding his head. When I got all through, he asked me, "And has your father quit drinking?"

"Just beer, I think."

"Has he hurt you anymore, since you came here to Mr. Kreimer's?" he asked.

"No."

"Do you have any idea of how much beer your father had had just before the accident?" Blanca asked.

"I only saw him drink two."

"Boomer, you've told me before that you're only afraid of your father when he's drinking. Weren't you afraid when you saw him drinking the beer?" Blanca asked.

"No." I shook my head. "He was acting all right. I don't think he's drinking much any more. I looked in the trash barrels and there weren't any whiskey bottles."

Blanca gave Mr. Harris a funny look, then started on another track. "Boomer, why do you think your mother left your father?"

I wasn't sure what I should say.

"Tell us, Boomer," Mr. Harris said, "why did your mother leave and go live someplace else?"

"Because sometimes when Dad drinks he hits her and punches her," I said.

"He hurt you, too, Boomer," Blanca said, looking straight in my eyes. "Why didn't you go with your mother when she left?"

"Because I couldn't take my dog, Sunny."

"Was that the only reason?"

"No. I guess I kind of wanted to stay with Dad, too. I knew he'd be okay if he wasn't drinking. And most times, when he'd been real mean, he'd be real nice for a while. I figured me and him could get along okay."

"You did?" Blanca said, like she was waiting for me to say more.

"Besides, I didn't want Dad to be all alone. I figured he needed me, kind of like I needed Sunny," I said.

Blanca turned toward Mr. Harris. He looked down at some papers he had in his hand. Then he looked up over the top of his glasses at me and asked, "Would you want to live with your father again if he wasn't drinking, Boomer?"

"Yes sir, Mr. Harris, I would. As long as he's not drinking. When he's not drinking, my dad is the best dad in the world."

Mr. Harris didn't say anything for a while. He just looked at me until I was beginning to get nervous. Finally he said, "Thank you, Boomer."

Afterward, Bud told me that Mr. Harris is a probation officer and he is the one who will recommend to the judge what they should do about Dad. I keep wondering if I should have told the plain truth like that. I hope I did right.

Mom called me at Mr. Kreimer's that night. I asked her if maybe she wouldn't come back up to our house again. She cried and said she didn't know. I will hope for the best. For a while it seemed like I would never get my cast off, but I did. So maybe things will work out with Dad and Mom, too.

Saturday, May 29

What a surprise! No wonder Dinah was so big—with two babies in her. She didn't know herself that she was going to have twins until the last couple of weeks.

She named them Margery and Virginia. I asked her why she didn't give them names that were alike. She says they will be enough alike in other ways without having almost the same names.

She was only in the hospital a couple of days. When she first came home with the babies, they were kind of funny-looking. But

when I saw them
this morning,
they looked a
lot better. I
guess babies
are like puppies,
they get cuter as
they get older. Dinah let me hold one. I think it
was Margery. She grabbed my finger with her
little hand.

But the best thing of all is that I'm back
home! Dad isn't drinking—not even beer. Mom
moved back two weeks ago and I've been back
home since last weekend.

Dad pleaded guilty to reckless driving and
driving without a motorcycle license. Mr.
Kreimer and Bud and me and Mom went to
court to watch. The judge really gave Dad a
talking to about how lucky he was. "First of
all, you're lucky you didn't kill yourself or your
son. And if your son had sustained any injuries,
you'd be going to jail for felony reckless driving
or worse!"

He stopped, like he wanted to be sure Dad

was taking it all in. Then he said, "Second of all, you're lucky your blood alcohol level was below the limit. Otherwise you'd be facing a mandatory jail sentence."

Then he turned his head and looked straight over at me when he said, "But the luckiest thing of all is this probation report. You've got a very loyal son who loves you and wants you home in spite of what you've done to him. Because you have a fine boy who wants his father, I'm giving you one more chance, Mr. Nichols. Don't blow it!"

So the judge said he was going to put Dad on probation, and he had to pay a fine. He can't drink even beer and he has to go to A. A. at least twice a week. So Dad and me and Bud go together on Saturdays. While they go to the regular A. A., I go to Alateen. And almost every night, on the way home from work, Dad stops off there while Mom does the shopping.

Blanca, from the county, is going to visit me here at my house. Bud and Mr. Kreimer invited her to stop by whenever she has time.

I think she likes Mr. Kreimer and she is crazy about Bud's cakes and pies. No wonder she is so fat.

Sunny is home with me, too. I gave Spunky to Mary Margaret, even if it wasn't her birthday yet. Her folks already have a couple of dogs, but they are outside dogs and live in the barn with the horses. Mary Margaret says their father was a wild dog that lived in the canyon where she and Patrick used to live. Spunky is her pet dog and sleeps in the house.

The pigs are still at Mr. Kreimer's, but Dad and I are building a pen for them so we can bring them up here. Mary Margaret and I are thinking of keeping the gilt (that's what they call girl pigs) and raising pigs for our next 4-H project, and just butchering the barrow (that's the boy). Dad says he will help me build a little shelter for the gilt and the babies. Except that she'll be a sow, instead of a gilt, after she has babies. Mom says pigs make flies and she doesn't want anything to do with them.

Later, when we were out in the barn, Dad

told me, "Don't worry about Mom. She's a sucker for any kind of baby. One look at little piglets and she'll change her mind about pigs."

"If she's so crazy about babies, why don't we have one?"

"Who knows, maybe we will. A lot of things are going to be different around here." He put both arms around me and hugged me close. "I'm not going to blow it this time, Boomer." His voice sounded like he might be crying.

I hope we do have a baby. Since Dad quit drinking he and Mom are getting along real good, and we have plenty of room at our house for a baby.

This next Saturday, we are going shopping for a dirt bike. Mr. Kreimer saved half of the money Dad paid for my keep and gave it to me toward the motorcycle. With the $45 every month from Grandma's money, I have almost enough for a brand new dirt bike. Dad says he will pay the rest if I will let him ride it sometimes. I said he can ride it anytime—if he wears a helmet and gets a motorcycle license if he's going to ride it on the street!

Mom is making molasses cookies. They sure smell good. She got the recipe from Dinah. Now that Dad's quit drinking, he eats lots of cookies and pies and cakes. Mom is busy all weekend baking enough to last us through the week.

I'm pretty busy, too, helping Dad with the pigpen, so I probably won't write anymore in this journal. Besides, my friend Jake is going to be here in a couple of weeks. He's going to get a motorcycle, too, so I won't have time to write anymore. We'll be too busy riding.

Dinah made a book out of the journal that Jake wrote last summer. She called it JAKE'S JOURNAL. She asked if she could

read mine and maybe make it into a book, too.

I don't care if Dinah reads it, but putting it in a book is different. I wouldn't want to hurt Dad's feelings. I told him I was sorry I'd had to tell Mr. Kreimer and everybody about what happened. "Maybe I shouldn't let Dinah put it in a book for everybody to see."

Dad put his arm around me. "Don't be sorry, Boomer. You did the right thing. I wish you'd told Mr. Kreimer, or even somebody at school, sooner."

"But what about putting my journal into a book? That's different, Dad. It would be embarrassing for people to read about what happened."

"It will be worth it if it encourages some other kid with our kind of problem to ask for help. I'm learning to face up to the truth about myself, even when the truth hurts. So tell Dinah to go ahead. Just as long as it's the truth, Boomer."

And that's what it is.

About the Author

R. E. Kelley's first story for children, published in 1985 by *Ranger Rick* magazine, was selected as the best published story for children in 1985. She has been writing for children ever since.

The author—whose full name is Ruth E. Kelley—grew up in a small village near Buffalo, New York. Back then, there were only a few radio programs for children, and no television at all. In the summertime she could play outside and go swimming in Murder Creek, which ran through her backyard.

In the cold snowy winters, she read and read and read. Some of the stories she read were so good she read them many times. Some were so awful she promised herself she would write better ones when she grew up. But it wasn't until after her son and daughter were grown that she started writing.

She wishes that she'd kept a journal when she was young, to help her write her stories now. She still remembers, though, how much she wanted stories to seem real, so that is how she writes.

She lives in a canyon in California that is very much like the Freel Canyon in her first book, *Jake's Journal*. Many people who read it wanted to know more about Jake's friend Boomer, so she wrote *Boomer's Journal* for them.